Hotel Transylvania 4 Movie Novelization

Written by Genndy Tartakovsky
Adapted by Patty Michaels

Simon Spotlight
New York London Toronto Sydney New Delhi

This book is a work of fiction. Any references to historical events, real people, or real places are used fictitiously. Other names, characters, places, and events are products of the author's imagination, and any resemblance to actual events or places or persons, living or dead, is entirely coincidental.

SIMON SPOTLIGHT

An imprint of Simon & Schuster Children's Publishing Division

1230 Avenue of the Americas, New York, New York 10020

This Simon Spotlight edition July 2021

Copyright © 2021 Sony Pictures Animation. All Rights Reserved.

All rights reserved, including the right of reproduction in whole or in part in any form.

SIMON SPOTLIGHT and colophon are registered trademarks of Simon & Schuster, Inc. For information about special discounts for bulk purchases, please contact Simon & Schuster Special Sales at 1-866-506-1949 or business@simonandschuster.com.

Book designed by Claire Torres

The text of this book was set in Caslon Antique.

Manufactured in the United States of America 0521 OFF

10 9 8 7 6 5 4 3 2 1

ISBN 978-1-5344-9680-4 [pbk]

ISBN 978-1-5344-9681-1 [ebook]

CHAPTER 1
PARTY TIME!

It was an exciting night at the Hotel Transylvania. It was the hotel's 125th anniversary, and there was a major celebration planned! The ballroom was festively decorated with balloons and streamers. Monster and zombie guests started to arrive, dressed in their most ghoulish best. It was going to be one of the best celebrations at the hotel.

Mavis's husband, Johnny, roller-skated happily around the center of the ballroom while

Mavis; their son, Dennis; Mavis's dad, Drac; and his wife, Ericka sat at a table near Johnny.

"Here's to Hotel Transylvania!" Johnny exclaimed. "Celebrating one hundred and twenty-five years! Congratulations, Drac!"

Drac gave Johnny a polite smile. He loved his son-in-law, but sometimes Johnny could be a bit too . . . enthusiastic.

"So great. Thank you, Johnny," Drac replied. "What a wonderful surprise that was. I was so *full* of the enjoyment. Now we can move on to the actual *planned* part of the celebration."

"That was only the beginning, Drac," Johnny replied. "It's time you take a step back and enjoy your anniversary party!"

"What?" Drac asked.

"Relax, Dad," Mavis told her father. "Johnny

worked so hard to make this extra special."

"Oh no," Drac sighed.

"It's a Johnny takeover celebration!" Johnny shouted. "Just sit back, relax, and enjoy your party! Hit it!"

Just then, loud dance music started playing. Whatever Johnny had planned, it was surely going to be outrageous.

Drac's friends Wayne, Murray, and Griffin all looked at Johnny strangely. Like Drac, they thought Johnny was sometimes just a bit too outlandish. They looked over at Drac in curiosity.

"What are you looking at?" Drac asked his friends. "The show's *that* way."

"It's more fun to watch you squirm," Griffin replied.

From out of nowhere zombie fire dancers

appeared! They were dressed in hula skirts and spun fire sticks high into the air.

Suddenly Johnny shouted, "Let's do it, Frank!" At that moment Drac's friend Frankenstein appeared. He was juggling chain saws while riding a unicycle.

"Isn't this great?" Frank shouted. "Johnny taught me!"

"Send in the dogs!" Johnny yelled.

"Dogs?" Drac questioned.

At that moment a monster dog parade trotted in.

"Ice sculpture, go!" Johnny said. Zombie staff members of the hotel wheeled in a huge ice sculpture of Drac. The ice sculpture was gigantic! The bottom of it had been scooped out and filled with festive party fruit punch.

"Wolf pups!" Johnny called out. A swarming pack of wolf pups ran in. They were each holding a letter to try to spell out the words "Happy Anniversary." The letters were out of order, though, so Johnny's plan didn't exactly work.

After that, true chaos started to ensue. Frank spotted the fire sticks flying through the air.

He got very nervous. "Fire bad!" Frank shouted. He tossed the three chain saws he was holding, which flew in different directions. One chain saw hit Drac's ice sculpture. Another cut one of the zombies' arms off. The last chain saw set a curtain on fire.

"Okay, that is it. Hold it!" Drac yelled. He flew up into the air and used his powers to freeze everyone at the party.

"Dad!" Mavis shouted. He wasn't able to

freeze Mavis, because she was a vampire, just like Drac.

"Right, can't freeze other vampires," Drac grumbled. He turned to Mavis. "Look at this mess. It's a disaster!" He walked over to all the fires, blew them out, and started to fix the other messes that Johnny had created.

"Johnny did this all for you!" Mavis told him.

"You mean he created this chaos all for *me*," Drac replied sarcastically. "Wow, thank you, dear son-in-law."

"You know you love him!" Mavis said. "You're just keeping all your real feelings bottled up inside your coffin."

Mavis continued. "When Johnny came into our lives, he changed our whole world. In fact, you could really say Johnny changed everyone's world. He forced the monsters out of the shadows and into the humans' hearts."

"Well, technically they already accepted us, and we just didn't know it," Drac said defensively.

"Whatever, Dad. You can think what you want, but I know Johnny has made our lives complete, and I wouldn't change a thing."

"Okay, okay, whatever you say. Now let's continue this special day, 'cause it's going to get even *more* special," Drac said.

"What are you up to?" Mavis asked Drac suspiciously.

"What? Me? Nothing!" he replied. He used his vampire powers to unfreeze everyone.

The chaos in the ballroom had been fixed, and it now looked festive and organized just like it had looked earlier.

Drac addressed the crowd. "Thank you! Thank you, everyone!" he shouted. "And remember, precisely at midnight I will make a special, once-in-a-lifetime announcement!"

Mavis looked over at her dad curiously. What was he planning?

CHAPTER 2
A SECRET SURPRISE

Drac stepped outside onto the balcony. He wanted to collect his thoughts before he made his announcement.

Ericka joined him outside. "Woo-hoo! You ready for your speech?"

Drac sighed. "Yes, I think so . . . But UGH! Johnny is giving me the GREATEST headache of my entire existence right now. Like a giant wooden stake right through my brain!"

"Oh, you know Johnny," Ericka told him. "He just gets a little carried away."

"Yes, *exactly*," Drac replied. "That's the problem!"

"Well, you're going to have to get used to things being done a little differently when you retire—" Ericka began.

Drac quickly cut her off. "Shhhh!" he told her. He didn't want anyone to overhear the news—especially Mavis, who had super bat hearing!

"Not so loud," Drac whispered to Ericka. "Mavis can hear everything!"

"Why would she be listening?" she responded. "Don't be so paranoid!"

"I'm sure you're right," Drac whispered again. "I just don't want to ruin the surprise. For so long

I have dreamed of giving the hotel to Mavis."

"And Johnny," Ericka added.

"Yes, and Johnny," Drac reluctantly agreed.

"It is a big step. I know how much this hotel means to you," Ericka said.

"Yes, but it is time to let go and start a new chapter . . . together," Drac replied.

"You are just all sorts of wonderful, aren't you," Ericka said, smiling.

"It's not for nothing that they call me 'Count Wonderful,'" Drac replied jokingly.

But little did they know that Mavis *had* overheard what Drac had said. Her bat hearing was *very* sharp.

"Holy rabies!" Mavis said to Johnny. "You're never going to believe it!"

"What's going on?" he asked.

"Johnny, you'd better sit down for this," she said.

"You're freaking me out," Johnny told her.

"Dad is going to retire and leave us the hotel to run!" Mavis revealed.

Johnny sat quietly as he processed this information. Then he grabbed his chair and started to bounce up and down! "Yahoo!" he shouted.

Guests at the party looked over at him, bewildered as to what he was yelling about.

"He's okay," Mavis told them. "He had too much sugar today."

Johnny tried to regain his composure. "I didn't even know he was thinking of retiring," Johnny said.

"I didn't either," Mavis said.

"Oh my gosh, Mavis, I'm so happy for you!

You're going to be amazing!" he told her.

"You mean *we're* going to be amazing," Mavis responded. "Now, we can't spoil the surprise."

"And you know what this means?" Johnny said. "I'm *finally* part of the family!"

"What are you talking about?" Mavis asked. "You're already part of the family."

"I know, but you know how Cranky Fangs is sometimes," Johnny replied. "It feels like I am, but not really."

"That's not true," Mavis said.

"Well, not anymore, it isn't!" Johnny said.

"Shhhhh," Mavis told him. "We can't spoil the surprise. I can't believe Dad is actually going to do this!"

"Right, right, right," Johnny said. "I better walk this off." He walked away excitedly, talking to random monsters and zombies, who had no idea what he was happy about.

"Nothing to see, nothing much to talk about . . . except the greatest thing happening in the entire universe!" Johnny shouted.

Just then Johnny spotted Drac walking backstage. "Oh, there he is! Hey, Drac!" Johnny started to chase after him, but then stopped himself.

"Whoa! Nope, keep it cool, Johnny. There will be plenty of time to thank him after," Johnny said to himself. He grinned. This was going to be one of the best nights of his life!

CHAPTER 3
CHANGE OF HEART

Meanwhile, Drac was pacing back and forth backstage, rehearsing his speech.

"Dearest family, friends, and honored guests. I have started a new phase in my life, and I feel it is time to begin a new chapter for Hotel Transylvania . . . ," Drac began. He summoned a box and removed the key to the hotel.

"So, I am extremely proud and honored to give the key to the hotel to . . ."

Suddenly Johnny burst into the backstage area. He had tried to sit back in his chair at the table and stay calm, but it hadn't exactly worked. His chair was vibrating excitedly and shook all the way up the stairs, and landed right next to Drac! "Dad! I can't believe it!" he exclaimed.

Drac tried to speak, but Johnny wouldn't let him.

"I can't believe it!" Johnny shouted. "I am going to explode into a thousand little excited bits, and then those little excited bits are going to explode into millions of tiny little excited bits!

"Oh, mighty king, it is with all my heart that I accept this great honor," Johnny said. He grabbed the hotel key and waved it in the air like a sword. "With this mighty key, I will unlock the future, and usher in a new destiny for the great Hotel Transylvania!"

"Whaaaa," Drac said, bewildered. "How did you—"

"I have so many great ideas," Johnny replied. "I'm dizzy with hospitality creativity! Like, horizontal escalators all through the lobby! Name tags for all guests, for more casual relations. Green energy-saving options! Stationary bikes in every room for your own power source. It's going to be the ultimate Johnny takeover!" he exclaimed.

Drac imagined what his beloved Hotel Transylvania would become. He pictured the hotel lobby totally redecorated with a new age vibe. The zombie bellhop uniform would change to a long, flowing caftan. Ska musicians would perform surrounded by guests lounging on beanbag chairs, while other guests would do yoga in the lobby. A neon marquee outside the hotel would read HOTEL JOHNNY. . . .

"It's going to be the ultimate Johnny take-over!" Johnny repeated.

Drac realized he couldn't hand the hotel over. There would be too much change, and way too fast. He waved his hand in the air and froze Johnny.

I can't do it! Drac thought. *I thought I could give the hotel to Mavis and Johnny, but he's going to ruin everything! I have to get out of this!*

Suddenly Drac had an idea. He waved his hand in the air again to unfreeze Johnny.

"Whoa, whoa, whoa. I think there has been a

misunderstanding," Drac said. "I am not giving my hotel to you."

"But Mavis said...," Johnny began. He looked down sadly. "Oh, I get it," he said.

Drac quickly interrupted him. "No, no, no! It's not what you think. See, I actually *can't* give you the hotel!"

"What?" Johnny asked.

Drac thought fast. "It's because of a very old, ancient, *very serious*, real estate law," he lied.

"Real estate law?" Johnny asked.

"Yes, yes!" Drac replied quickly. "It said no residence, whether it be residential or commercial, shall ever be transferred to, owned by, or inherited by a human. For if it did, to wit, then that property shall be forfeited and repossessed!"

"Whoa," Johnny replied. "Those are some very serious "it's.""

Drac patted Johnny on the back, trying to make him feel a little better.

"I am truly sorry," he told Johnny. "I would absolutely LOVE to give you the hotel, but you know, you're not a monster, so . . . I can't."

"But then what's the big announcement?" Johnny asked.

Drac remained quiet for a moment. He realized he didn't know what he was going to say now.

What was he going to do now that everyone at the party was expecting a grand announcement?

CHAPTER 4
THE BIG ANNOUNCEMENT

Drac realized he didn't have much time to think about what he was going to say. Just then the stage curtains opened, revealing the cheering audience!

Ericka leaned over and whispered to Mavis. "Excited for the big announcement?"

Mavis smiled to herself. Little did Ericka know that Mavis already knew what Drac was going to tell everyone! "You have no idea," Mavis replied.

Drac nervously approached the podium. *Think, think,* he said to himself. *You've got to announce something!* He tapped on the microphone, sending feedback screeching through the ballroom. The audience cringed.

Just then a disappointed-looking Johnny sat next to Mavis.

"There you are!" Mavis said. "You almost missed it!"

Meanwhile, the audience started to wonder when Drac was going to say . . . anything! Frank, Murray, Wayne, and Griffin, part of the Drac Pack, looked at each other curiously.

"Boy, is he nervous," Frank said.

"Something's going on," Murray added.

"This is hard to watch," said Wayne.

"Get on with it!" Griffin yelled.

"Griffin!" his wife, Eunice, scolded.

"What?" he replied. "This is nerve-racking!"

"I know, but you have to be respectful," she told him. But then, she too lost her patience. "GET ON WITH IT ALREADY," she shouted.

Drac cleared his throat. "Dearest family, friends, and honored celebrants. I have started a new phase in my life . . . ," he began.

Mavis leaned into Johnny. "Here it comes!" she said happily.

"And I feel now is the time for Hotel Transylvania to, uh—uh—uh . . . ," Drac stammered.

His eyes nervously darted around the room. He spotted Mavis smiling back at him, and Ericka giving him a thumbs-up. Out of the corner of his eye, Drac spied Blobby drinking a pitcher of water, which caused Blobby to expand. *That's it!*

Drac thought. "Expand!" he shouted. "Yes, we are expanding the hotel!"

"What?" Mavis and Ericka asked incredulously.

"Yes, yes!" Drac explained. "In order to address the increasingly long lines, I am pleased to announce we will be adding a new restroom to the lobby! People come to the hotel, they've traveled long distances. They need to wash their hands, they need to use the facilities, they can't wait to get into their rooms. But what if the rooms aren't ready? Blah, blah, blah, now they will not have to wait to freshen up. I hope you all are as excited as I am for this, this totally official, *not*-made-up news!"

The audience reluctantly started to clap. It wasn't the most exciting news, but it *was* news.

Mavis was confused. "But I thought I heard...," she began.

This is all my fault, Johnny thought dejectedly. *I've got to find a way to fix this.*

Drac smiled faintly at the crowd. "So, let's get on with the party! Take it away, boys!"

Just then Blobby began to deejay. He started to play a popular dance song. Everyone rushed to the dance floor and started to boogie.

Mavis quickly approached her father. "Dad! A new restroom in the lobby? Really? There wasn't anything else you were going to announce?"

Drac tried to avoid her questions. "No, of course not! Hey, listen to that dope-tastic beat!"

He spun around the dance floor and managed to hide himself in the crowd.

Something doesn't sound right, Mavis thought. She scoured the crowd to try to find Drac again.

All at once, Drac bumped into Ericka. "What happened?" she asked. She was not pleased.

"Ericka sweetheart?" Drac shouted. "It's hard to hear, the music is so booming, and yeah, okay, feel that bass!" He quickly danced away from her and weaved through the crowd.

CHAPTER 5
THE TRANSFORMATION

"This is all my fault," Johnny muttered to himself. "I've ruined everything, all because I'm *not* a monster."

Little did Johnny know that someone had just overheard what he'd said to himself about not being a monster.

"So, you want to be monster, huh?" someone asked. "I can help with that. I've got just the thing down in the lab."

Johnny looked up in surprise. It was Van Helsing! If Van Helsing could turn him into a monster, then he and Mavis could run the hotel!

A few minutes later Johnny and Van Helsing entered Van Helsing's lab. The lab was very cluttered and disorganized. Van Helsing began to look through different boxes and bins.

"So, why are we turning you into a monster today?" he asked Johnny.

"Because of the monster real estate law," Johnny replied. "It says that no human can inherit a monster hotel, whether it be commercial or residential, or said property will be forfeit and repossessed unto it."

Van Helsing looked at Johnny curiously. "Huh," he said. "That's a new one." He continued to sift through the boxes. "Hmmm, it must be in the back somewhere." He walked through a giant maze of assorted junk. Johnny struggled to fit through the narrow passages of the lab. But then, he lost sight of Van Helsing in the maze of boxes and inventions.

"Hello? Van Helsing?" Johnny called out.

"Aha! I found it!" Van Helsing suddenly shouted. His arms popped out from the boxes. He was holding a giant ray blaster with a large crystal above the barrel. "Behold—the Monsterification Ray!" he announced. "It turns any human into a monster!"

"Awesome!" Johnny exclaimed. "Is it safe?"

"Hmmm . . . great question," Van Helsing replied with a shrug. "What we need is a guinea pig to try this out on!" He spotted his actual guinea pig sitting in her cage.

"Meet Gigi," Van Helsing said.

"Aw, she's so cute," Johnny commented.

"Not for long," Van Helsing replied. He switched the ray from "human" to "monster" and fired a red beam toward Gigi. The ray blasted Gigi, transforming her into a giant guinea pig the size of a dog! She now had massive teeth and very disheveled fur.

"Wow!" Johnny exclaimed. "Sign me up for teeth like these!"

Gigi growled and tried to bite Johnny's finger.

"And she has *seven* eyes!" Johnny shouted. "And laser vision . . ." He was so excited that he might be able to have all of the monster powers that Gigi now had!

"It doesn't work that way," Van Helsing explained. "Who knows what sort of hideous beast you'll become! So, let's see, shall we!" he said temptingly. He aimed the ray at Johnny.

Don't worry, Mavis! Johnny thought. *This is going to fix everything.* "Lay it on me, bro!" he told Van Helsing.

Van Helsing blasted Johnny with the ray. But nothing happened. Johnny looked down at his still-human body, confused. *Huh?* he wondered. A few moments passed, but still nothing happened.

All of a sudden Johnny's body started to contort. "Ugh, I don't feel so good," he muttered. Just at that moment a tail burst out behind him, and giant monster feet exploded through his sneakers. His hands transformed into two massive green hands with sharp, pointy claws. His teeth turned into fangs. But he still looked a bit like himself, as his hair was still red.

Van Helsing's eyes widened. "Ooh!" he commented. He was impressed.

Immediately, Johnny grew larger. He smacked into Van Helsing, causing him to fly out of the room. Johnny's monster shadow began to grow even bigger. He stood up straight and let out a monstrous . . . *ROARRRRRR!*

CHAPTER 6
THE MONSTER IS LOOSE!

Back in the hotel ballroom, Drac continued to weave through the dancing crowd, doing his best to avoid Mavis and Ericka. He ducked under a buffet table to hide.

Phew, he thought. *Safe at last!*

But that quiet moment didn't last very long. Just then, he heard a distant roar coming from what sounded like the basement. Drac grew a bat ear to hear the noise better, and listened with his ear pressed against the floor. He heard monstrous roars and crashes. The noises *were* coming from the basement. *That's where Van Helsing's lab is,* Drac thought nervously. *What is going on down there?* He managed to run out of the ballroom without being noticed, and headed downstairs to the lab.

"Hello? Van Helsing?" he called out. "Everything okay in here?" Drac heard a low growl in response. "Is anybody there?" Drac asked nervously.

He peered into the area of the lab where the growl was coming from. Boxes started to shake, and the growling grew louder. Just then, the source of the growling rushed toward where Drac was standing!

Drac gulped nervously.

Suddenly two large, clawed hands appeared

from behind the boxes. It was . . . Johnny, who was now a monster!

"Hey, Drac! What's up?" he asked casually.

Drac's eyes widened. "Johnny?" he asked incredulously.

"Yeah, it's me!" Johnny replied. "I'm a monster!" He spun around in a circle clumsily, almost knocking Drac to the floor with his tail. "Check out these big feet! And these claws. Oooh, and these ears. They are so pointy! And look! I've got a tail!"

"What? Ho— Why did you— How did you—" Drac stuttered.

"It was totally easy! I just used Van Helsing's monster ray! Now you can give the hotel to Mavis and me just like you wanted!" Johnny smiled widely, showing off his new set of fangs.

"Mavis is going to LOVE the new me!" Johnny continued. "Let's go show her!"

"Wait, wait, wait!" Drac called out. Johnny ran past Drac and accidentally tripped Drac with his tail, causing him to crash into a pile of items on the floor. Johnny burst through the door and ran down the hallway.

"Mavis!" he called out.

Drac scrambled to get up. *Oh no*, he said to himself. *Mavis is going to kill me.* Then he spotted the ray. He picked it up and looked at it curiously. He turned the dial to "human," and the color changed from red to green.

"Yes!" Drac shouted. He ran upstairs to find Johnny.

Meanwhile, Johnny was lumbering through the corridors upstairs in the hotel, looking for

Mavis. "Mavis!" he shouted. "I've got great news!"

Drac had come upstairs and spotted Johnny. He fired the ray toward Johnny, hoping to turn him back into a human. The ray missed, and hit a zombie bellman instead!

The zombie turned into a human! "I can't believe it!" the bellman shouted. "I'm human again!"

Another zombie bellman rushed over and bit him. He hadn't lasted as a human for long!

"Oops, I'd better be careful," Drac said. "There are monsters everywhere!"

Drac continued to chase Johnny. He attempted to shoot another ray at him. The ray shot past Johnny and through an open window into the ballroom! The ray ricocheted through the crowd and hit the ice sculpture of Drac. The ray was absorbed into the punch at the bottom of the sculpture. The punch turned an ominous shade of green and began to bubble wildly.

Oblivious to the chaos around her, Mavis spotted her uncle Frank. "Have you seen my dad?" she asked him.

"Nope, not since the announcement," Frank replied, chewing a mouthful of food.

"Huh, now that I think about it, I haven't seen Johnny in a while either. Where *are* those two?" she wondered.

At that moment, Johnny turned a corner in one of the hallways and ran right into Dennis and Winnie! They were busy playing with a group of furry, bouncy, barking monster dogs.

"Hey, Dennis!" Johnny called out.

Dennis looked at Johnny strangely. "Daaaad? Is that you?"

"Yeah!" he said. "Isn't it great? I got to go show your mom!"

Drac charged into the hallway and fired the ray toward Johnny, who ran off in the other direction. The ray missed him again!

"Papa Drac, was that my dad?" Dennis asked.

Drac stopped dead in his tracks. He suddenly hypnotized both Dennis and Winnie.

"That was not your father, Dennis," he said. "It was just a random monster. Everything is normal."

Drac's hypnosis worked! "Okay. Everything is normal," the two children replied.

At that moment, Johnny had finally almost reached the ballroom. "Mavis! I have great news!

Whoa," he shouted. Just then, he tripped over his giant monster feet right before he could enter the ballroom. He tumbled into an open elevator. Drac spotted him and fired another shot from the Monsterification Ray. But the doors closed, and the ray missed Johnny yet again.

"Argh!" Drac yelled. He turned into a bat and flew to the top floor, where he waited for the elevator to open. As the doors opened to reveal Johnny, Drac aimed and fired again. This time the ray hit the back of the elevator and ricocheted back toward Drac, and hit *him*! Suddenly Drac was catapulted out of the window. As Drac fell, he transformed back into his vampire form. He tried to turn back into a bat, but it wasn't working. Then he slowly started to transform, but this time into a ... human! His pointy ears started to shrink, and his fangs turned into normal-sized teeth!

"Oh no, something's wrong!" Johnny yelled. "Don't worry! I gotcha, Dad!" He launched himself out the window. He had to save Drac—and fast!

CHAPTER 7
A CLOSE CALL

Meanwhile, Wayne, Frank, Murray, and Griffin were in the ballroom enjoying their desserts when they heard a giant *SPLASH!* They looked out the window to see what the commotion was.

They spotted Drac falling into the pool, with Johnny following right behind him. Johnny landed in the pool in a giant cannonball! "Wah-hoooo!" Johnny yelled.

Drac and Johnny didn't realize that Murray,

Frank, Griffin, and Wayne had heard the noise. They ran to the pool to investigate.

"Hey, guys!" Johnny said.

The group looked at Johnny in shock. "Johnny, is that you?" Murray asked.

"Yep, it's me!" Johnny replied. "Pretty great, right?"

"What happened to you?" Frank asked.

"Where's Drac?" Griffin pressed.

Suddenly everyone spotted Drac high above them. He was hanging from a window ledge. He must have climbed up when everyone was distracted by Johnny. But just then, he slipped and fell!

"He's not turning into a bat!" Frank shouted.

Murray quickly turned into a sand tornado and reached Drac as he fell toward the ground.

They both landed safely. Drac stood up slowly, revealing his human form!

"Drac?" Frank asked incredulously.

Drac spotted his reflection in a glass door. "No!" he shouted. "It can't be!"

"Whoa, look at us, Drac!" Johnny exclaimed. "You're human, and I'm a monster. It's like Freaky Friday on a Tuesday!"

Drac frantically looked around for the Monsterification Ray. "Where could it be? Where is it? It's got to be here somewhere!"

"What's going on, Drac?" Frank asked.

"I need to find the ray!" Drac cried.

"You mean that one?" Murray asked. It was sticking out of a zombie's eyeball! Drac pulled the ray out of the zombie's eye socket and aimed the ray toward himself. But . . . nothing happened.

"Come on, come on! Why isn't this working?" Drac shouted.

Johnny looked at the ray. "I think it's broken," he told them. Sure enough, there was a giant crack in the crystal.

All at once, they heard Mavis nearby. Johnny wanted to tell Mavis his great monster news, but Drac knew better. He faked being in pain.

"Drac! Oh my gosh, what do we do?" Johnny asked.

"Take me to Van Helsing's lab!" Drac hollered. He turned to his friends. "Do not tell Mavis," Drac told them. Then he continued to fake an illness. "Ow! The lab, Johnny! Oh, ow, hurry!"

Oh, okay! I gotcha, Drac!" Johnny said. He picked Drac up and carried him to the lab.

"Hey," a voice suddenly said a few moments later. It was Mavis! She was standing right behind the four friends.

"Was that my dad?" she asked.

"No," Frank quickly said.

"*Definitely* not your dad," Wayne added.

"Abso-lomunitely . . . not!" Murray stammered.

Mavis was instantly suspicious. "What is going on?" she demanded.

"Uh, Wayne wanted to show us a new dance move!" Griffin quickly said. Wayne started to perform a series of silly dance steps. His friends joined in.

Mavis was confused, but her dad's friends *did* act weird sometimes. "Well, if you see my dad, please tell him I need to talk to him," Mavis said, giving them a strange look and walking away.

"Sure, yep," they answered together.

Murray, Wayne, Frank, and Griffin all let out a sigh of relief. Their Drac-turned-into-a-human secret was safe—for now.

CHAPTER 8
MONSTER CHAOS

Johnny and Drac had just arrived at Van Helsing's lab. Van Helsing had the ray hooked up to an intricate contraption to run some diagnostics on it. Johnny was still cradling Drac.

"Well, it's broken," Van Helsing confirmed. "The crystal has cracked and is beyond repair."

"What?" Drac said. "Then get a new one!" He leapt out of Johnny's arms.

"These crystals are VERY rare and hard to

come by," Van Helsing reported. "It took me three years to find that one! I was but a young monster hunter at the time and—"

Drac cut him off. "Okay, don't need the whole story," he said.

Van Helsing shot Drac an annoyed look. "But luckily, I was brilliant enough to install a crystal locater on the ray itself, just for this situation," Van Helsing finished. He held up the ray, and switched on a lever. It beeped with a loud ping, and a hologram of a globe suddenly appeared. Van Helsing pointed to South America on the globe. "There it is, Drac!" Van Helsing shouted. "The crystal is in a cave in South America."

"South America?" Drac replied.

"Oh, cool!" Johnny exclaimed. "I was there once spelunking with some Norwegian wrestlers. We can just pop down there and get a new one!"

"If only it were that simple," Van Helsing said. "You will have to overcome the most perilous obstacles to then face the horror of the REFLECTION!" he continued. "Be fore-warned, for in your reflection the guardians shall awaken, and you will face an unspeakable evil." He turned around, pointing. "It cost me my right back wheel."

Drac and Johnny looked to where Van Helsing was pointing. The back wheel on his gray iron body was now a sparkly purple wheel.

"Uh . . . sorry for your loss?" Drac responded politely.

Van Helsing tossed the ray to Drac and walked off. "Happy hunting!" he told him.

"This is a disaster!" Drac cried.

"Don't worry, Drac! We'll get you back to your old self," Johnny said. "But first I'd better tell Mavis we're going!"

"What? Oh no, no, no! You can't tell Mavis!" Drac said.

"Why not?" Johnny replied.

Drac thought quickly. "She will want to come with us! And I was thinking this could be a fun father-son bonding trip. You know, just the two of us."

"Awesome!" Johnny shouted. "We can send her a postcard!" He gave Drac a giant, monster-strength hug.

"Okay, time to go," Drac instructed. "We have no time to waste!" He jumped into the air like he usually would when he was turning into a bat.

He fell to the ground with a loud *thump*.

"Right, still human," he grumbled.

Back in the hotel ballroom, the party had just ended. The ice sculpture of Drac had almost melted. But the punch that had turned green was still actively bubbling.

Frank, Wayne, Griffin, and Murray were walking through the ballroom.

"Such an improvement," Frank commented.

"Yeah, I think Johnny looks way better as a monster!" Wayne added.

"The green really brings out his eyes," Murray said.

Just then, Frank's phone beeped with a text

message from Drac. Frank sighed loudly as he read it.

Going to find crystal, to fix ray, to turn us back to normal. DON'T TELL MAVIS! the message said.

Frank and his friends didn't like to get caught between Drac and Mavis, but they were hoping Drac would turn back into a vampire before she ever found out.

"This stinks. I hate covering for Drac," Wayne said.

"What should I write back?" Frank asked.

"How about 'No! We're not covering for you anymore,'" Murray suggested.

"Yeah, how about, 'Now that you're human, you can do nothing about it!'" Griffin said.

"Go do your own dirty work for a change!" Wayne added.

Frank started typing. "Okay, got it!" He hit send.

"What? You actually sent that?" Wayne asked.

"Oh man, we're in trouble now!" Murray complained.

"Nah, I sent him a GIF of a dancing cat!" Frank showed his friends the silly image. Just then, Frank spotted their friend Blobby. "Hey, Blobby, pal . . . check it out!"

Blobby looked at the image on Frank's screen. Suddenly Blobby transformed himself into a Blobby-jelly version of a cat and started dancing!

The friends all grabbed a glass of punch. Frank made a toast. "Here's to dancing cats!" he cheered. They all took big gulps of the punch.

A few moments later, Murray's green, glowing eyes started to flicker. He blinked, and his eyes turned into human eyes! What was going on?

"Uh, guys, something is happening," Murray shouted. Then his mummy bandages started to loosen. He looked over at Wayne the werewolf, who started to shed his long hair. Wayne then noticed that Griffin the Invisible Man's nose was starting to appear. Then Frank's stitching started to come apart, with his body parts starting to disconnect! Soon their transformations were completed. They had all turned into humans also! But the worst transformation of all had happened to Blobby, who had just taken a sip of punch. He had shrunk down from a giant green blob to a . . . plate of gelatin! What were they going to do *now*?

CHAPTER 9
DRAC'S FIRST FLIGHT

Meanwhile, high up in the air, a tiny airplane spurted and sputtered, with smoke billowing off one of the wings. Johnny hung his head out the window, his tongue flapping in the wind. Then he yanked his head back inside.

"Flying as a monster is so much better! Right, Drac?" Johnny asked.

But Drac was not having the same kind of exciting experience. He was very nervous and hyperventilating into a bag. He was used to flying as a monster, not as a human!

"How is this plane even in the sky?" Drac cried. "What's that sound? Do you smell burning? Is that duct tape holding the wing together?" He looked out at one of the airplane wings, which was indeed held together with duct tape. The wing promptly fell off.

"Okay, folks," one of the Gremlin pilots announced. "We've reached our cruising altitude. We're not expecting turbulence. So, sit back, relax, and enjoy the ride."

Drac looked around and breathed a sigh of relief. He relaxed into his seat.

But the quiet didn't last for long. Just then, the Gremlin pilot yanked the steering up and down. The plane started to rock violently from side to side. The monster passengers sat calmly and undisturbed as Drac was thrown back and forth! Then he started to turn green.

"Hey, Drac, I think you're turning back into a monster!" Johnny said.

"No, I'm getting nauseous," Drac said. He stumbled toward the bathroom.

"Aw, are you feeling sick?" a Gremlin flight attendant asked. "Try spinning!"

She grabbed Drac by the arm and spun him around. But that just made his nausea worse!

"Maybe something to eat will settle your stomach?" she asked. She handed him a plate of slimy seafood and eyeballs.

Drac was about to be sick when the attendant offered him some fresh air. She tied a rope around his legs and opened the latch on the door labeled EMERGENCY EXIT. Suddenly the door flew off, and Drac was sucked out of the plane! He flew out the opening still tied to the rope, and flailed helplessly.

"Aaahhhh," Drac yelled.

Johnny calmly yanked him back in. "No worries, Drac," he said.

Hours later, the plane safely landed at an airport in South America. Johnny's backpack appeared on the luggage carousel with a loud *thump*. Suddenly the backpack started to move and Drac's head popped out of it.

"Was this really necessary?" Drac asked.

"They'd never let you in without a passport,"

Johnny told him. Drac quickly hopped out of the bag, hoping no one had seen him.

"Whatever. Let's get going!" Drac ordered. They headed outside into the bright sunlight. Drac looked up at the sun in terror. "The sun!" he cried. He panicked and hid in his own large trunk for safety.

"Uh, Drac, the sun won't fry you now," Johnny told him. "You're human, remember? It's totally safe."

Drac realized that Johnny was right. Since Drac was no longer a vampire, the sun no longer posed a threat!

"The sun . . . ," Drac began. "It's . . . magnificent! I cannot believe that my whole life I have missed this elegant splendor. It's glorious, it's wondrous, it's, it's . . . it's BURNING MY

EYES!" He tried to shield his eyes, but the sun had temporarily blinded him. He staggered into the busy street, and narrowly missed being hit by moving vehicles.

"Drac!" Johnny yelled. He rushed into traffic, trying to save him. Just then, Drac stepped into the path of an oncoming bus! Johnny's monster arms reach in and pulled Drac to safety.

"Don't worry. I got you," Johnny said. "You stay here. I'll get us a taxi," he told Drac.

But as he tried to whistle to hail a taxi like he usually would have, flames shot out of his mouth! He was becoming more and more monster-y.

For a moment, he had forgotten he was a monster.

"Sorry! I didn't know I could do that," Johnny

said. "But don't worry. Taking the bus is going to be even MORE fun."

Drac loved Mavis, and he wanted her to be happy. He doubted she would love the new Johnny. And Drac hated being a human. He loved being a vampire. He missed being his old handsome self, and being immortal!

Drac sighed. *When is this nightmare going to end?* he wondered.

CHAPTER 10
THE TRUTH IS REVEALED

Back at the hotel, zombies and witch maids were cleaning up after the party. Drac's four friends, who had now turned into humans, were nowhere to be found.

A zombie was vacuuming in front of a big plant. As the zombie passed, Frank's head suddenly popped out.

"I don't get why we are hiding," Frank complained.

"If Mavis sees us, she's going to know something is up! It's best to avoid the whole situation," Wayne said.

At that moment, Mavis and Ericka bumped into each other.

"Have you seen my dad?" Mavis asked.

"Have you seen your dad?" Ericka asked at the same time.

"Here's our chance," Wayne hissed. "Let's get out of here!" The foursome had started to sneak away when they realized that they'd almost forgotten Blobby.

Just then, Mavis and Ericka noticed the group. But they had no idea who the people were!

"Who are you?" Mavis asked.

"It's me, your uncle Griffin," Griffin said. "What, you can't recognize me?"

"No! I've literally never seen you before!" Mavis yelled.

"Well, we're all here," Murray said.

"Uncle Murray?" Mavis asked.

"In the flesh!" Murray responded.

"Uncle Griffin? What is happening?" Mavis demanded.

"Okay, don't panic, but it's me, Uncle Wayne," Wayne said.

Ericka looked at the group in confusion. "Let me get this straight. Griffin?"

"Yep," he responded.

"Murray?" she asked.

"I think so," Murray said.

"Frank?" she asked.

"You know it," Frank said with a wink.

"Eunice?"

"It's me," Eunice said.

"Wanda?"

"Hello!"

"Mavis, what is going on?" Ericka asked.

"That's what I would like to know," Mavis replied.

Just then, Frank's phone beeped with a message. He swiped his screen to show a live video news report.

The newscaster announced, "This just in from our international desk. This was the scene outside a local South American airport, where an unidentified monster saved a confused man dressed up in a Halloween costume."

Mavis peered at the screen. "Dad!" she shrieked. Then she looked at the screen again. "Wait! That kind of looks like Johnny!"

"Yep, your dad's human and Johnny is a monster. Wait . . . I don't think I was supposed to say anything, but I can't remember," Murray blurted out.

"Drac is *human*?" Ericka asked.

"Johnny is a *monster*?" Mavis asked.

"How in the world?" Ericka asked.

Suddenly a loud crash interrupted them. Gigi, who was still a gigantic guinea pig, burst into the room. Van Helsing ran behind her, trying to put her leash on.

"Grandpapa!" Ericka shouted. "You're responsible for this, aren't you?"

Van Helsing sighed. "To be honest, Johnny asked to become a monster, and Dracula being human was more of an . . . accident. And I'm afraid I have some more bad news. Looks like

69

the transformation keeps mutating, and won't stop until the monster part has taken over the human part completely!"

"We have to get to them!" Mavis cried.

"I have just the thing," Ericka said. She headed outside to the Van Helsing blimp. Mavis; Frank; Eunice; Griffin; Wayne; Murray; Wayne's wife, Wanda; and the wolf pups piled in. Griffin was holding Blobby on a plate. Ericka sat in front of the captain's wheel of the blimp and launched the blimp into the air.

"I just don't understand why Johnny would turn himself into a monster in the first place," Mavis said.

"Your dad's going to have a LOT of explaining to do," Ericka replied. "He's a human now?

That's ridiculous, not to mention much less attractive."

"Don't I know it!" Mavis said. "My cute human husband is now a monster. My adorable vampire father is now a human! What is going on with everybody?" She looked at all her dad's friends. Nobody said a word. Blobby just sat on his plate and jiggled.

MONSTER PETS

PETS

A HOTEL TRANSYLVANIA SHORT

CHAPTER 11
MOSQUITO TROUBLE

Back in South America, Johnny and Drac were on a local bus, which was slowly traveling through the dense jungle.

"Ugh, why are we moving so slow?" Drac complained. He looked out the window and noticed that the back of the bus was literally dragging on the ground because of Johnny's monstrous weight! Drac took out the ray and saw the tracker beeping, but it was barely moving.

"You see, Johnny, your monster-ness is all over the place, weighing us down, and we're getting nowhere!" Drac shouted.

Johnny stuck his head out one of the bus windows to see what Drac was talking about.

Then he had an idea. "I know just what to do!" he exclaimed. He popped his head out of the top of the bus. His legs shot out of the bottom of the bus. Then his arms popped out of the bus's windows on both sides! He grabbed the bus and stood up and started running, carrying the bus with him!

Drac rolled his eyes. But then he noticed that the tracker of the ray was getting closer to their destination, so maybe Johnny's idea wasn't so bad after all!

Later that day, Drac and Johnny were walking through the jungle on their way to find the exact location of the crystal. Although Johnny had no trouble walking through the thick branches and leaves, Drac kept getting caught on thorns and sticky branches.

"We're getting nowhere fast!" Drac complained.

"It's your tuxedo and cape," Johnny said. "They are not good for trekking." He started pulling clothes out of his backpack. Soon Drac was outfitted in a brand-new hiking outfit! A Hawaiian shirt, cargo shorts, a floppy hat, bulky socks, and hiking boots completed the look.

"We're twinsies!" Johnny exclaimed.

As the day wore on, Drac grew more and more

tired from the hot sun and strenuous walk. He was so thirsty! A few minutes later, he spotted a beautiful waterfall.

"Well, that looks refreshing," Drac said happily.

"Oh, I don't know, Drac," Johnny began. "Once, in Thailand, my friend Khamatchka and I—"

Drac sighed in frustration. "You have a story for everything, huh?"

"Well, yeah, I traveled a lot," Johnny said. "I would have never found your hotel if it wasn't for my adventurous spirit and lust for life!"

"And that would have been *terrible*," Drac said sarcastically.

"I know!" Johnny said earnestly.

Drac couldn't resist the waterfall any longer. He took off his hiking gear and jumped into the water with a giant splash, wearing only underwear. Immediately Drac leapt out of the water. He was covered in flesh-eating piranhas!

"Aaghhhhh!" Drac yelled.

A little while later, Johnny had helped Drac cover his wounds with bandages and they were back on the hiking trail.

"Look on the bright side," Johnny said encouragingly. "You're not hot anymore!"

"Right," Drac replied miserably. "I've traded one somewhat manageable annoyance for an excruciatingly painful one."

Johnny didn't get the joke. "Yep! That's the spirit, Dad!"

Drac and Johnny continued their trek. Drac was getting more and more tired, until finally, his legs just collapsed.

"Soooo tired," Drac whispered. "Body shutting down. Eyes need to rest."

Johnny warmed up a pot of coffee with his fire breath.

"Here, Drac, you just need a little wake-me-up boost of caffeine."

Johnny poured the whole coffee pot into Drac's mouth. Drac chugged it down.

"I don't feel anything," Drac said sleepily.

Then . . . POP! One eye opened, then the other. Drac leapt up, fully energized!

Drac was on a full coffee explosion of energy.

He started racing around, noticing everything.

"Hey! Wow! Look at that tree!" Drac shouted. "Those flowers are lovely! What a colorful bird! Ants! This is fun! I can't blink!!!"

But just a little while later Drac was exhausted again, while Johnny was having a blast. "I am loving this new monster me!" he cheered.

"I agree with you there," Drac said. "This human business, I just don't know how you can function!"

"Well, I think it's how you look at it," Johnny said.

"Right, you're always looking on the bright side," Drac remarked.

"Yeah! If you were still a monster, we wouldn't be able to be here because the sun is out," Johnny told him.

"Well, you are right about that. If I never became human, actually, we would never have even gone on this trip and we would not be in this situation," Drac said.

"See, *now* you're getting it!" Johnny exclaimed.

Drac sighed once again. He wasn't getting through to Johnny at all. And just when Drac thought the day couldn't get any worse . . . it did. Just then, Johnny and Drac encountered a giant swarm of mosquitoes! They did their best to swat them away.

"Gah! They are everywhere!" Drac cried. And because mosquitoes weren't able to bite monster skin, they were only attacking Drac!

At that moment, a giant mosquito landed on Drac's cheek.

"Oh no! I got this one, Drac!" Johnny shouted.

As he tried to helpfully swat the mosquito away, he accidentally punched Drac, causing him to fall to the ground. He had accidentally knocked Drac unconscious!

CHAPTER 12
A SIGNAL DETECTED

A while later the Van Helsing blimp arrived in South America. Now that they were in the jungle, they were going to need a different type of vehicle to look for Drac and Johnny.

"We're going to need to take this to the ground," Ericka told the group.

Luckily, she had just the thing. Suddenly they all appeared in a giant truck and burst out of the back of the blimp! "Woo-hoo!" she yelled, zipping through the trees. As they plowed through the jungle, the truck suddenly hit a big bump!

All the human monsters flew out of the truck and landed on the ground! Mavis quickly turned into a bat and zipped around, catching everyone and putting them back into the vehicle.

"Thanks, Mavis," Murray said.

Ericka checked the truck's tracking equipment. "I can't seem to pick up their signal," she reported.

"Let me try," Mavis urged. She put on her cloak to shield her from the sunlight and transformed her ears into bat ears to take a better listen.

Suddenly she picked up a signal. It had worked!

"Got them. This way!" Mavis cried.

"Well, that was supercool!" Ericka exclaimed.

Mavis was excited that she had picked up the signal, but she was also nervous.

"Don't worry," Ericka reassured her. "We'll find them and turn them back to normal. Besides, your dad is with Johnny, and he'll watch over him." She thrust the truck into high gear, and they sped through the jungle.

Little did they know that all was not going well for Drac and Johnny. Johnny was still trekking through the jungle while carrying Drac, who was still unconscious.

A few minutes later, Drac started to awaken!

"Good morning, sleepyhead. Have a good nap?

That's a fun, human-y thing to do!" Johnny said cheerfully.

"Nap?" Drac yelled. "You slapped me so hard, I lost consciousness!"

"But I *did* get that mosquito," Johnny said.

"Where are we?" Drac asked.

"Just following the ping," Johnny replied.

Drac looked at the ray-crystal locator. "Hmm, okay, it seems like we are getting closer," he said. But as he watched it, the ping faded . . . and then disappeared!

"Hey, what is going on?" Drac shouted.

Just then the mist cleared, revealing they were on the tip of a very high mountain ridge.

Drac gulped nervously. Where were they?

"Whoa, we're really high up," Johnny commented. "What a weird place to find a cave."

"That's because you've been going the wrong way!" Drac yelled. "I can't trust you to do anything right!"

Johnny, who had still been carrying Drac, put him down on the ground. Suddenly, Drac felt very off balance.

"Drac, are you okay?" Johnny asked.

"No, I feel woozy," Drac said.

"It must be the elevation," Johnny told him.

"That's ridiculous!" Drac said. " I can ... fly ..." But because Drac was now a human, he couldn't fly anymore. He lost his balance and fell off the cliff! Johnny, trying to grab him to safety, also lost his footing and fell off the cliff! As Drac and Johnny fell from the sky, Drac noticed something on Johnny's back.

"What? Johnny, you have wings!" Drac cried.

"I do?" Johnny responded. "Cool!"

"Cool? Cool? The ground is getting closer every second! Fly us down to safety!" Drac yelled.

Johnny tried to fly, but his wings didn't work. "I don't know how to use my wings!" Johnny yelled back.

"Just trust yourself!" Drac said. "Now move those wings!"

Johnny tried, but he couldn't move them at all. "It's not working!" he cried.

"You're trying too hard!" Drac shouted. "Wiggle your nose and your toes. Now . . . FLAP . . . YOUR . . . WINGS!"

Johnny listened to Drac's instructions. Suddenly his wings started to flap and he was able to fly! He sped toward Drac, and grabbed him just before he was about to hit the ground!

"Woo-hoo! Wow, Drac, you really know your monster stuff!" Johnny cheered.

"A lifetime of experience," Drac said with a sigh of relief.

CHAPTER 13
CAMPFIRE CONFESSION

Later that night, Drac and Johnny had recovered from their near-death experience and were roasting marshmallows around a campfire.

"Boy, that was fun!" Johnny said.

"Right," Drac replied sarcastically. "Getting lost and almost falling to your death is *super* fun."

"See, you're doing it again!" Johnny responded. "Always looking at something in the *worst* possible way. I mean, if we never got lost, you'd never have fallen, and I wouldn't have realized that I have wings and could fly. Now we got to bond, and in no time, we'll get to the Crystal Cave!"

Drac sat quietly for a moment as he ate a melted marshmallow. "Who knew something so strangely gooey could be so sweet and delicious? This is truly one of humankind's finest achievements!"

"It's a perfect example!" Johnny exclaimed, grabbing a marshmallow and toasting it. "At first a bland squishy pillow. Then . . . oh no! It's on fire and horrible—seemingly ruined! But blow out the fire and bite into it, and sweet goo melts in your mouth and warms your very soul."

"Maybe I'm like this because of the centuries of persecution," Drac realized. "All the hate, the worry, the loss . . ." He thought for a moment. "You know, raising a daughter—you're constantly worried, always fearing the worst," Drac admitted.

"You did a great job," Johnny told him. "Mavis turned out amazing! I'd marry her in a minute," he joked. "This is nice. We never get a chance to do stuff together. You know, just the two of us." He lay back and looked up at the sky. "The stars were just like this when I found your hotel," he said. "My whole life changed that night."

"Hmm. I guess. Hard to remember so long ago," Drac replied.

"My whole life changed that night," Johnny repeated.

"Mine too," Drac agreed.

"Who knew it would become my new home?" Johnny asked.

"I definitely never would have guessed that in a million years," Drac responded.

"Mavis, you, the guys, and the hotel. You're my *real* family," Johnny said.

"Heh, it all means so much to you?" Drac asked.

Johnny grinned. "Of course! That's why I became this awesome monster. I know how much the hotel means to you. It feels like that for me and Mavis, too. No monster real estate law is going to stop that!"

Drac thought that maybe it was time to tell Johnny the truth about the hotel. But a loud roaring sound of an engine suddenly interrupted them!

BOOM! Ericka pulled her truck directly in front of them! Mavis and Johnny spotted each other first.

"Mavis!" Johnny cried out.

"Johnny?" Mavis said in disbelief. "I see you. You're still in there, aren't you?"

"Of course," Johnny said.

"Mavis? Ericka? Wanda? Eunice?" Drac asked. "Who? What? Huh? Frank?"

"It's us, and we're human just like you," Griffin told him.

Mavis turned to Johnny. "Why did you turn yourself into a monster?" she asked him.

"So we can keep the hotel in the family," Johnny told her. "You know, because of the monster real estate law!"

"I don't understand," Mavis said.

Ericka glared at Drac. "Yes, me neither," she said. "Could you explain it?"

"Well, see—" Johnny began.

Drac cleared his throat. "Okay, wait. Let me, please. Well, it all happened so fast," he began. "Johnny overheard me say that I was giving you guys the hotel. But then he . . . you know, had a Johnny takeover—escalators, name changes. And, well, . . . I panicked!"

"And LIED," Mavis said accusingly.

"Wait," Johnny said in confusion. "There is *no* monster real estate law?"

Mavis turned to Johnny and said sweetly, "And then *you* turned yourself into a monster because you know how much the hotel means to us."

Johnny grew upset. "Yes. But wait. That means this was all a lie? I'm here on this trip not because

Drac wanted to have some bonding time with me. I'm here because Drac needs to turn me back to a human so he would not be able to give me the hotel. Which was all a lie to begin with!" He was growing increasingly angry.

"Johnny, no. Look, I didn't mean—" Drac began.

"So, the only real truth is that *you* never wanted me here, there, or anywhere!" Johnny told Drac.

"Dad? How *could* you?" Mavis said.

Just then, Johnny tried to say something, but instead of words, it came out in a loud . . . roar! He was having trouble talking in human language. Now he was talking monster!

"Oh no!" Mavis cried.

"Johnny, wait!" Drac pleaded.

"*ROARRRRRR!* Johnny out of here!" he

shouted. He stomped away into the jungle, angry and alone.

"I hope you're satisfied!" Mavis yelled at Drac. "Everything Johnny does is to try to make you and me happy. But you can't see that, can you? You never did, and you never will! I don't want your stupid hotel! When we return, we're leaving!" Mavis flew away to find Johnny.

CHAPTER 14
JOURNEY TO CRYSTAL CAVE

Everyone stared at Drac.

"Come on. We have to find the crystal and fix the ray," Ericka said quietly. "Johnny doesn't have much time left."

"What do you mean?" asked Drac.

"There's a time limit to his humanity. We have just a few hours left before the transformation is complete. Once fully transformed, he can never return to human."

"Oh no!" Drac said.

"Everybody, back in! Let's go!" Ericka yelled.

Drac took out the crystal tracker. It showed the direction they should travel in. "Through there!" he shouted. As they traveled on, a terrible tropical storm approached! Torrential rain started to pour.

Drac checked the tracker again. "Follow the river!" he yelled.

Ericka pushed a button and shifted some gears without reducing her speed. Drac didn't realize he had directed Ericka right off of the road! But without missing a beat, Ericka transformed the jeep into a an aquatic vehicle in midair! She smiled as she stepped on the gas and accelerated through the rapids.

Drac looked at the radar, and it directed them

straight ahead into a cave entrance that had a frightening skeleton face.

"Ooh, scary!" Griffin said.

"Yes, that's it. Go there," Drac told Ericka. She quickly guided the boat toward the narrow entrance of a cave. The river current slowed down as they approached the jagged rocky teeth of the cave opening. Ericka realized that the opening was *really* narrow.

"Everyone, down!" she instructed.

While everyone else was about to enter the cave, Mavis was searching for Johnny. She spotted some red hair on a tree branch and followed it to a section of trees that had been knocked over.

Traces of red hair were everywhere. Suddenly she noticed a giant, flying creature. It was Johnny, who had turned into a gigantic creature the size of a dinosaur!

Just then her phone rang. It was Ericka. "Mavis! We found the Crystal Cave!"

"Oh my gosh, that's great! I'll get Johnny to follow me. I'm coming!" Mavis said. A map popped up on Mavis's screen, directing her to the location.

"So mad at Dracula!" Johnny shouted.

Oh no, Mavis said to herself. She tried to remain calm. She flew directly in front of his face so he would recognize her. "I want to help you. We need to turn you back to yourself!"

"No!" Johnny shouted. "No one want Johnny. No Johnny Human. No Johnny Monster!"

Johnny yelled. "Johnny be with Johnny!" He let out a roar and started to chase Mavis.

"No, I love Johnny no matter who you are on the outside," Mavis cried.

"No! Must love Johnny. Inside! Outside! *ROARRRRRR!*"

The only thing left for Mavis to do was fly as fast as she could away from Johnny.

CHAPTER 15
THE RED CRYSTAL

Back in the cave, it was eerily dark. The beeping flashing light from the tracker illuminated Drac's face.

"We are close," said Drac. He remembered Van Helsing's message: "The guardians shall awaken, and you will face an unspeakable evil. . . ."

The boat continued to sail through the cave. Suddenly, sharp stalactites dropped from above!

The water began to boil as lava fountains started to erupt. Then it became pitch dark.

"Well, that wasn't that bad," Drac commented.

Just then, the tracker changed color and started to beep even louder.

"I'll go first," Drac told the others. Drac walked deeper into the cave alone. He saw his reflections everywhere in the crystals. He gasped and told everyone to follow him. Everyone was thinking the same thought: Would they be able to save Johnny in time?

Johnny continued to chase Mavis. And not only that, but the sun was starting to rise, which was bad news for a vampire like Mavis!

Meanwhile, everyone else looked around the Crystal Cave. It was dazzlingly beautiful.

"This doesn't seem so scary," Drac said. "Van Helsing made such a big deal about this place. 'Be forewarned, for in your reflection the guardians shall awaken,' and blah, blah, blah . . .

"Whoa," Drac said suddenly. "It's so strange to see my reflection. . . ."

"Drac?" Ericka asked, walking over to him. "Is it any one of these crystals? Or is there a special one?" She looked at him strangely. Something about him seemed . . . different for some reason.

"How am I supposed to know? Do I look like some kind of crystal expert?" Drac snapped.

Ericka looked at Drac strangely yet again. It

was not like him to speak in that tone of voice.

"Whoa, really?" she replied.

"We're never going to find it, so let's just get out of here!" he yelled.

In another area of the cave, the real Drac picked up a crystal and tried to put it into the ray.

"Ugh, doesn't seem to work," he complained.

"Well, that doesn't fit, so we better go. I don't think it's here," the other Drac replied.

"We can't give up that easy. It must be here somewhere," the real Drac argued.

"Nope. You're wasting your time," the other Drac answered.

Suddenly, Ericka approached and saw both Dracs. "I knew there was something not right about this," she said.

Drac sensed something strange also. It was

like he was talking to himself—out loud!

And in fact, he was, because his reflection was a complete replica of himself. Now there were two Dracs—and one didn't seem to be very nice at all.

"The reflection!" Drac realized. Van Helsing's warning had been right. He realized it was his own reflections that had become the guardians of the crystal.

Ericka gasped. "Your reflections in the crystals—they've somehow come alive and are trying to stop us from getting the crystal!"

"You'll never get your hands on the crystal!" evil Drac said.

Just then, Drac and Ericka heard screams from other parts of the cave. "Drac—no!"

"Stop!"

"What are you doing?"

"Noooo!"

Ericka and Drac came to a horrible realization. There wasn't just one evil Drac. There were others!

CHAPTER 16
EVIL DRACS

Just then, Mavis swooped through the cave. She had to be careful to avoid falling stalactites and shooting lava. She ran into Drac—but little did she know that it was one of the evil versions of him!

"You're too late!" the evil Drac shouted. "You need to leave! Bye now!"

"What?" Mavis asked in bewilderment. "You're acting funnier than usual."

"Nothing to joke about. No crystal here, so ya gotta go!" evil Drac said.

Then, Mavis heard yelling and saw what appeared to be yet another Drac run by!

What is going on? she wondered. Suddenly she spotted hundreds of evil Dracs running around, trying to hurt her family and friends!

Mavis quickly knocked one of the Dracs down but lost her cloak in the fight. Three more ran toward her.

At that moment, the *real* Drac saw her fighting. "Mavis!" he yelled, running to help her.

But Mavis couldn't tell the difference, and punched him!

"Ouchy!" the real Drac yelled.

"Dad? Is that really you?" Mavis asked.

"Yes. Look, I'm bleeding," Drac replied.

"Fascinating." He smiled at his daughter.

"What is happening?" Mavis demanded.

"My reflections have come alive and are trying to stop us from getting the crystal. But you've come back! You're not mad anymore?" he asked his daughter.

"Of *course* I'm still mad, but I needed to turn Johnny back to a human!" she replied.

"Wait, where is he?" Drac asked.

At that moment the roof of the cave was completely swiped away by a massive, two-hundred-foot-tall JOHNNY-zilla! He bellowed loudly.

All at once, Mavis spotted a red glow. "Wait, is that it?" she shouted.

Drac looked toward the glow. He noticed it was the exact same shade of red as the crystal that powered the ray! Mavis leapt to grab it, but multiple evil Dracs tried to stop her.

She pushed them away, but just then a bright ray of sunlight hit one of the stalactite crystals in the cave and bounced off it, hitting Mavis!

"The sun!" she cried. "I can't get to the red crystal!"

"But I can!" Drac shouted.

"What about all of the other Draculas?" Mavis shouted.

"I will not let myself stand in the way of my family's happiness!" he yelled. "It's Drac take-over time! Sorry about this, Blobby." He grabbed some of Blobby's gelatin and spread it onto his feet, which allowed him to skate around on the floor of the cave. He continued to punch and duck away from his evil selves, and grabbed the red crystal! He tossed it to Mavis.

Mavis was trapped. There was just too much sunlight. She fell to her knees, trying to protect herself. Suddenly a shadow enveloped her. Then she heard a familiar voice.

"Hey, kiddo."

Mavis looked up to see Frank standing over her.

Mavis smiled gratefully.

"Thanks, Uncle Frank!"

Frank nodded. "We've got you covered. Literally."

Eunice looked around. "What's everyone standing around for? Go go go!"

The wolf pups and Wanda climbed up a crystal shard to make more shade for Mavis. Mavis turned into her bat form, held the ray, and flew as far as she could before she ran out of shade again.

"Okay, Griffin," Wanda shouted. "You're up!"

"All right," Griffin said. "Hold still, Wayne."

Griffin climbed up Wayne to sit on his shoulders.

"Gah!" Wayne complained. "Why do I have to be on the bottom?"

Griffin and Wayne cast their shadows toward Mavis. Mavis flew under them.

Eunice climbed on top of another crystal piece. Her hair cast a protective shadow toward Mavis. Mavis quickly flew to where Eunice was perched.

Eunice looked at Murray.

"Murray?"

But Murray was snoring.

"Murray!!!" Eunice yelled.

Startled, Murray woke up. "Huh? I'm awake!"

Eunice groaned. "Ugh, useless," she said.

Eunice sighed as she removed her head and threw it toward the towering ledge. Mavis followed the shady protection provided by Eunice's head's shadow.

Mavis put the crystal in the ray. The ray surged with energy. She switched the ray to human mode and pointed the ray toward Johnny. The ray hit Johnny in the face.

Mavis sighed with relief. "Yes!" she cheered.

But nothing happened. It didn't work. Johnny's eyes still flashed angrily at Mavis and Drac.

"Oh no," Mavis wailed. "We're too late!"

"No! There is still some Johnny left! I have to try!" Drac yelled. He skated up a ramp and headed toward Johnny. Johnny grabbed Drac in midair, his huge monster hands practically crushing him!

"Dad!" Mavis yelled.

As Johnny continued to roar at Drac, Drac spoke to him softly.

"Johnny," he said. "You are the marshmallow."

"Huh?" Johnny grunted. He looked down at Mavis.

"You were right," Drac continued. "You said that if I only saw the worst in things, I would miss the best parts. I was so worried that you would ruin everything I cared about that I didn't see YOU. Your kindness. Your energy. Your Johnnyness! Before you, my life was like a burnt marshmallow: hard, and crunchy, and sad. But you cracked it open and became the ooey-gooey center of all of our lives!"

Wayne leaned over to whisper to Griffin.

"Well, we're dead."

But Drac continued to look Johnny straight in the eye and kept talking softly to him.

"What I'm trying to say, Johnny, is that you ARE part of the family. My family. I'm sorry it took me so long to say it, but you taught me to look for the good in everything, and now I see that so much of the good in my life is because of you," Drac finished.

Suddenly Johnny's eyes turned back to normal. He looked at Drac with love. He was himself again, in his mind, anyway. Now he just needed to get back to his human size.

"Aw, Dad," he said. He gave Drac a giant hug.

"Now, Mavis!" Drac shouted. Mavis shot

Johnny with the ray. It worked! He transformed back into himself.

Mavis flew toward them as everyone rode out of the cave in the truck. Mavis switched the ray to MAKE MONSTER mode and zapped Drac. Drac transformed back into his normal self too!

Griffin, Wayne, Frank, and Murray wanted to be turned back into monsters too!

"Um, can I get some of that?" Griffin asked.

Mavis used the ray to turn all of them back into monsters.

A few minutes later, Drac approached Mavis and Johnny. "I wanted to say that if you want, entirely up to you . . . I would love for you BOTH to take over the hotel duties and do whatever you think is right to do."

"But I'm not sure if we could follow in the path

that you have set for us . . . ," Mavis began, "and, well, I've been thinking about this a lot, and we would love to, but . . . the hotel is you. How could it ever be *ours*?"

"No, Mavis. . . . The hotel is not just me. It's all of us," Drac responded.

"Even me?" Johnny asked.

"Of course," Drac said.

Johnny smiled at Mavis and Drac. He really *was* part of the family now!

CHAPTER 17
A HOTEL
TRANSFORMATION

Everyone was excited to get back to the Hotel Transylvania. But as they approached the gates of the hotel, they spotted a terrifying sight. The hotel was wrecked!

"We're home?" Ericka asked, in shock.

"Oh no!" Mavis yelled.

Van Helsing's giant guinea pig Gigi had destroyed the hotel! And what was even worse, it had trapped Van Helsing, Dennis, Winnie, and the hotel dogs on the roof! Ericka knew just what to do.

She grabbed the ray and pointed it toward the blimp. Suddenly a larger ray popped out. She blasted it toward Gigi. The ray zoomed through the air and hit Gigi, who transformed back to normal size!

"Yay!" everyone cheered.

Now that everyone was safe, Mavis and Drac felt relieved, but they were also so sad that the Hotel Transylvania was gone. They had made so many memories there.

But Johnny felt differently.

"This is incredible!" he shouted. "We will get to rebuild it exactly the way we want to. It'll be so cool! I'm already getting so many ideas! We should totally change the shape!

Like, make it an *H* or a giant *T*. Then we could do elevators on the outside. Oh, and inside they could go horizontally . . ." He trailed off.

"Those all sound great, honey. I'm just not sure Dad will approve," Mavis told him.

Just then, Drac appeared with luggage in his hand. "Do what you want. It's all yours! We're going on vacation," he cheered.

"What?" Mavis asked. "For how long?"

"I'm sure we will make it back for the grand reopening," Ericka told them.

"Cool! We'll get started!" Johnny exclaimed.

"Love you, Mavey Wavey," Drac told his daughter.

"Love YOU, Daddy-Wavey," Johnny said to Drac, beaming.

"Love you too, Johnny," Drac said. Drac was happy. He knew he was leaving the new hotel construction in good hands, *and* he was going on vacation! What could be better than that?

THE
END

Are you a Drac, a Johnny, or a Mavis?

Take this quiz and find out! Read each question, and then pick the letter of the answer that sounds most like you. Write your answers down on a separate piece of paper.

1. You're invited to a party. What is the first thing you think of doing?

A. Get a nice gift for the host and hostess. A fresh bottle of type-O blood would be perfect—it goes with everyone!

B. What is there to think about? It's a party! Woo-hoo! If anything, just think about the great time you are going to have!

C. Make sure you bring some great music. Everybody loves to dance—or fly! And keep track of the time. If you leave after sunrise, that may cause some problems!

2. How do you keep your better half (husband/wife, boyfriend/girlfriend) happy?

A. Do anything your sweetheart wants to keep them happy!

B. Keep your honey laughing—everyone likes to laugh, right?

C. Holy Honeymoon! Make sure your sweetheart knows you will support them no matter what wacky thing they do! Make every day feel like the first day you met!

3. Describe your fashion sense.

A. Classic and neat. Every hair must be slicked back in place. I haven't changed my look in two hundred years!

B. Funky and cool! I love wild colors and crazy combinations!

C. I like to wear things that are in style. Black is my favorite color. Black dress, black fingerless gloves, black nail polish, black lipstick. Did I mention I love black?

4. What makes you happy?

A. Flying!

B. Dancing and laughing!

C. Being with my family and friends, and travel!

5. How do you solve a problem?

A. I talk it out. I consider the situation, consider the alternatives, and yada yada, the answer usually comes to me while I'm thinking out loud.

B. I just do the first thing that comes into my head!

C. I love playing detective and figuring everything out. My friends say nothing gets past me!

6. What is one of your lifelong dreams?

A. To travel the world with my love.

B. To throw the world's best party!

C. To build a fabulous chain of hotels all around the world!

7. Finish this sentence. I hate . . .

   A. People who don't follow rules and tradition.

   B. People who never break rules and tradition.

   C. People who are mean to monsters, and monsters who are mean to people. I don't like to say "hate," but I guess I am just not a fan of anyone who is mean!

8. Imagine this: One of the customers at Hotel Translyvania says they did not enjoy their stay. What do you do?

   A. I would apologize, invite them to come back for a free weekend, and make sure to send a basket to their room full of our finest monster delicacies, like freshly fried eyeballs!

B. Dude! How could anyone not enjoy their stay at Hotel T? It's so awesome. I say bogus, but I would talk to them and try to find out what was really bothering them. Maybe I'd take them out dancing.

C. I'd throw the most awesome party, maybe a monster masquerade ball, and they would be the guests of honor. Everyone loves a party, even zombies and vampires! If that didn't work, I guess I'd give them a full refund.

9. Do you like change?

A. A little bit. I realize things have to change—every hundred years or so.

B. I love change! I get bored easily and would change everything every single day if I could!

C. I don't see why you can't have both change and tradition. Some traditions are cool, like birthday parties! But I like to switch things up once in a while too!

10. Name something that you love.

A. Family

B. An all-night dance-a-thon!

C. A beautiful sunset with my love!

IF YOU PICKED . . .

Mostly A's: You're a Drac! You're classy and cool and love to keep traditions.

Mostly B's: You're a Johnny! You're reckless and wild and love to try anything new that sounds like fun!

Mostly C's: You're a Mavis! You're chic and smart and funny and try your best to keep the peace and make sure everyone is happy!